New Year's Eve Thieves

Suddenly the kids all heard a noise outside. They looked up.

A face wearing a dark ski mask was staring through the window.

Nate screamed and Socks came running. He barked at the face in the window.

The scary face disappeared.

The kids ran to the window. They saw two guys running across [the] [ya]rd next door. The runners [disappeared be]hind the house.

Then the stra[ngers were stand]ng on the Duncans' snow[y yard.] The kids could see the men's b[reath a]s they talked.

"We should call your aunt and uncle," Brian said to Lucy. "Those guys are going to rob Dink's house!"

New Year's Eve Thieves

by **Ron Roy**

illustrated by
John Steven Gurney

SCHOLASTIC INC.

This book is dedicated to the Perenick boys.
—R.R.

To Fiorella
—J.S.G.

ISBN 978-0-545-81214-6

Text copyright © 2014 by Ron Roy. Cover art, map, and interior illustrations copyright © 2014 by John Steven Gurney. All rights reserved. Published by Scholastic Inc., 557 Broadway, New York, NY 10012, by arrangement with Random House Children's Books, a division of Random House LLC, a Penguin Random House Company. SCHOLASTIC and associated logos are trademarks and/or registered trademarks of Scholastic Inc.

12 11 10 9 8 7 6 5 4 3   15 16 17 18 19 20/0

Printed in the U.S.A.   40

First Scholastic printing, January 2015

Contents

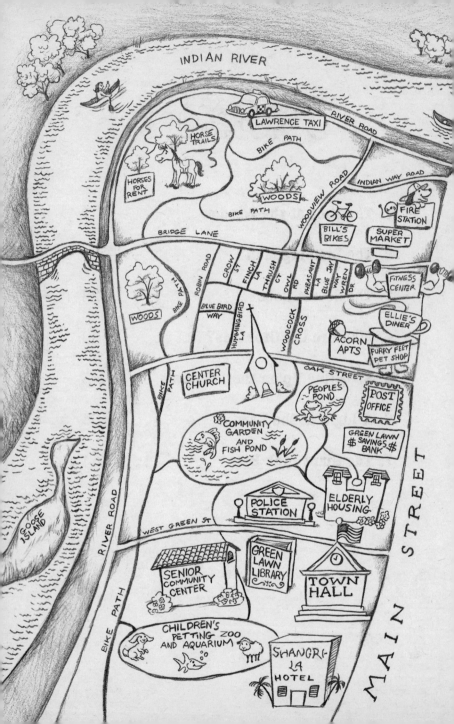

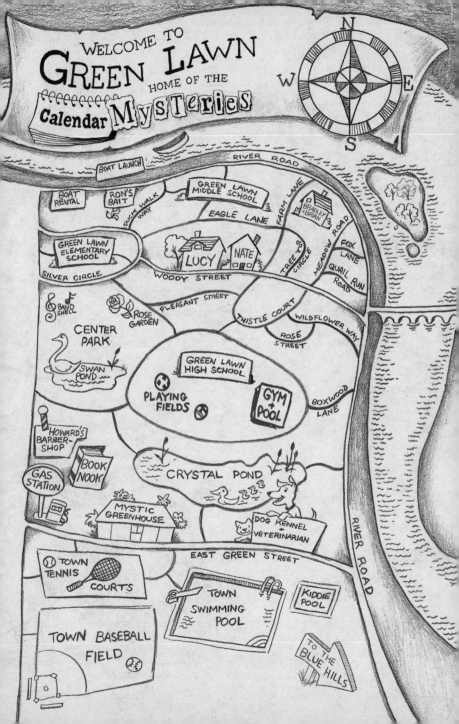

1

The Face at the Window

"It's your turn, Nate," Bradley said.

Bradley, Brian, and Lucy were at Nate's house, sitting on the floor around his Monopoly board.

Nate was petting his new puppy, Socks. "I know it is," he said as he reached for the dice. Suddenly Socks snatched a pile of play money and raced across the room.

Nate chased the puppy and trapped him behind a chair.

"Socks, give me the money!" Nate said in a stern voice.

Socks dropped the money and licked Nate's hand.

Nate grabbed the money. "Thank you, Socks," he said. "Good dog."

"Socks wants a toy," Lucy said. "Puppies need stuff to chew on."

"He chews my shoes all the time," Nate said. "And my mittens and my hat."

"But that's why he should have a toy," Bradley said. "You should get him something of his own to play with."

"Yeah, let's go buy him a toy," Brian added. "Mrs. Wong has lots of pet stuff in her shop."

The kids grabbed their jackets and headed out the front door.

"Be a good boy, Socks," Nate told his puppy. "And don't eat the money!" Socks flopped on the floor and wagged his tail.

The kids walked toward Main Street. Snow covered the ground and the tree branches. People on the street smiled at each other and said, "Happy New Year!" The big clock over the bank read 3:00 P.M. DECEMBER 31.

"The party at our house is at six o'clock," Bradley reminded the others. "But my mom wants us there before it gets dark. After we buy Socks his toy, we'll have time to go back to Nate's and finish the game."

When the kids walked into Furry Feet Pet Shop, Mrs. Wong was feeding the goldfish. "Hi, kids," she said. "How was your Christmas?"

"Mine was great!" Nate said. "I got a puppy from my sister."

Mrs. Wong smiled. "I know," she said. "Ruth Rose and I loved keeping it a big secret from you."

"How was your vacation in Florida?" Bradley asked.

"Most of it was wonderful," Mrs. Wong said. "But I dropped my cell phone into the ocean! It sank right to the bottom. And while I was away, my house got burglarized! A thief came in and stole my laptop computer!"

"Oh my goodness!" Lucy said. "Did you call the police?"

"Yes, and Officer Fallon came right to my house," Mrs. Wong said. "The only thing missing was the laptop. We don't know how the thief got in, because none of the doors or windows had been broken."

"I hope they catch whoever did it," Brian said.

"Me too," Mrs. Wong said. "I miss e-mail!"

Nate looked at the shelves of pet supplies. "I need a new toy for my puppy, Socks," he said.

"Lots of choices," Mrs. Wong said. "Does Socks want something soft and furry, or something rubbery that squeaks?"

Nate laughed. "He wants both!" he said.

Mrs. Wong showed Nate a purple rubber figure shaped like a big peanut. It had fuzzy green hair. "Then he should love this," she said. "He's called Mr. Purple." She squeezed Mr. Purple's belly, and it squeaked.

Mrs. Wong held the figure under Nate's nose. "Take a sniff," she said.

"It smells just like peanut butter!" Nate said.

"Yup. Dogs love peanut butter," Mrs. Wong told him.

"Perfect," Nate said. "How much is it?"

Mrs. Wong smiled. "Free. It's my Christmas gift to Socks," she said. She slipped the toy into a bag and handed it to Nate.

"Thank you!" Nate said. "I'll bring Socks over so he can thank you, too!"

The kids left the shop. It had started to snow, and the flakes landed on their hats and noses.

"We have a thief in Green Lawn!" Brian said. "I wonder if he's robbed anybody else."

Nate glanced around. "Look for someone with sneaky eyes," he said in a low voice as they walked back to his house. "He could be anywhere!"

Bradley laughed at Nate. "*Your* eyes look sneaky," he said. "Especially when you're trying to cheat at Monopoly!"

Nate threw some snow at Bradley, and the kids ran all the way back to Woody Street.

When Nate opened his front door, Socks was chewing on a comic book.

"No, Socks. Bad dog!" Nate cried. He took the comic book away and pulled Mr. Purple out of the bag. "Look what I got for you!"

Socks grabbed the toy and raced toward the kitchen.

"How's your comic book?" Lucy asked Nate.

"One page is ripped," he said. "But I can fix it with some tape." He walked to the desk near the window. After he found the tape, he looked out the window at the thermometer on the front porch. "Guys, it's down to thirty-seven degrees!" he yelled.

Their parents had told the kids they could sleep in the Pintos' barn in their sleeping bags after the party. "But only if the temperature doesn't go below freezing," they had added.

"I bet we can't sleep in the barn tonight," Brian said.

"But I love sleeping in your barn," Nate told Bradley and Brian. "Smelling the hay makes me think I'm a cowboy."

"And I like hearing our pony, Polly, snore," Bradley said.

"Best of all is the pigeons in the loft," Brian said. "They make these cool noises all night." He flapped his arms and said, "Coo, coo, COOOO!"

Bradley and Nate laughed.

"Well, if it's too cold to sleep in the barn, at least maybe we'll be allowed to stay up till midnight!" Brian added.

Lucy didn't say anything. She looked sad.

"What's the matter, Lucy?" Bradley asked. "Don't you want to have a party and a sleepover?"

Lucy sighed. "Sure, but my parents are going to miss my birthday," she said.

Lucy's parents were in Arizona helping to build a new school for Native American kids. They had been there for a year while Lucy stayed in Green Lawn with her cousin Dink and his parents.

"When is your birthday?" Bradley asked.

"January first," Lucy said.

"Cool!" Brian said. "That's tomorrow!"

Suddenly they all heard a noise outside. They looked up.

A face wearing a dark ski mask was staring through the window.

Nate screamed and Socks came running. He barked at the face in the window.

"It's the laptop thief!" Brian yelled.

2

The Limping Man

The scary face disappeared.

The kids ran to the window. They saw two guys running across Dink's yard next door. The runners disappeared behind the house.

"Did they have sneaky eyes?" Brian asked Nate.

"I couldn't tell," Nate said. "I only saw one face, and it was wearing a ski mask!"

"But why were they peeking in here?" Lucy asked.

"Maybe this house is their next burglary!" Brian said. "They were checking to see if anyone was home, and Nate's scream chased them away."

"Look, there they are again!" Brian said.

The kids watched the two strangers creep around the side of Dink's house.

One of the men was limping. He wore a cowboy hat, partly covering a long ponytail. The lower half of his face was hidden by a red bandana. A backpack hung from one shoulder.

The other stranger wore a ski mask. It had holes for his eyes and mouth.

Now the strangers were standing on the Duncans' snowy sidewalk. Then they walked up onto Dink's porch and peered through the window. The one in the ski mask said something to the one in the cowboy hat. The kids could see the men's breath as they talked.

"We should call your aunt and uncle," Brian said to Lucy. "Those guys are going to rob Dink's house!"

"Dink's parents aren't home," Lucy said. "They're at your house with your parents, getting ready for the party tonight. Dink, Josh, and Ruth Rose are there, too."

"Burglars always break in while people aren't home," Nate whispered. "Like at Mrs. Wong's house."

"Maybe we should tell Officer Fallon," Brian said.

"But we don't know if those are the guys who took her laptop," Lucy said. "They could just be tourists who got lost."

Nate laughed. "Tourists don't come to Green Lawn," he said. "There's nothing here for them to see! Besides, tourists don't put on masks and peek in people's windows."

The strangers started walking away. They left big footprints in the snow.

Bradley grabbed all their coats. "Come on. Let's follow them!" he said.

The four kids hurried out the door. The sun was behind the trees. It would be dark soon.

They stayed well behind the strangers. Up ahead, the two men were leaning together, talking. The one with the limp was tall. The other one was short. Their breath made little clouds. They walked down Woody Street, then Silver Circle, then passed Green Lawn Elementary School.

"Where do you think they're going?" Lucy whispered.

"They're headed down Main Street," Nate said. "Maybe they're planning to rob the bank!"

"Or Mrs. Wong's pet shop!" Brian said. "They already robbed her house!"

The bank and most of the shops were closed on New Year's Eve.

The two strangers passed the fitness center, then stopped in front of Ellie's Diner. Her lights were on, and a big sign in her window said OPEN ON NEW YEAR'S EVE.

The four kids hid behind a mailbox and a lamppost.

"They'd better not try to rob her!" Bradley said. "I heard that Ellie knows karate!"

"Maybe they're just going in for a hot chocolate," Lucy said.

The guy in the ski mask took a small camera from his pocket. He snapped a picture of Ellie's, and they both walked inside.

"Uh-oh," Bradley whispered. "Why do they need a picture of Ellie's?"

"Crooks like to study a place before they break in," Nate said. "They'll probably come back after she's closed."

"I'm going in," Bradley said. "I want to check out these guys up close."

"But they probably saw your face when they looked through Nate's window," Brian said. "If you walk into Ellie's, they'll know we're following them!"

Bradley was wearing a yellow ski hat that had holes for his eyes and mouth. He pulled it down over his face. "They won't know it's me," he said through the mouth hole.

"What are you going to do in there?" Brian asked.

"I'll just listen," Bradley said. "Maybe they'll say something about Mrs. Wong's laptop."

Bradley checked for traffic, then

scooted across the street. In front of Ellie's, he peeked through the glass. Or
tried to. The glass was foggy, and he
couldn't see a thing.

He made sure his face was covered
and walked in. The bell over the door
jingled. A silver banner over the counter
said HAPPY NEW YEAR!

The two strangers were at the counter. The one in the cowboy hat was hand-
ing Ellie some money. They each picked
up a take-out cup.

"Enjoy your hot teas!" Ellie told
them.

At least they're not robbing her, Bradley thought.

The men headed for the door, passing Bradley. They didn't even glance at
him. But he looked right at them. The
tall one had a tanned face and hands. A
tan in the middle of winter!

"Hi, Bradley," Ellie said. "Or is it

Brian? And why is your face covered?"

"It's Bradley," he said. "Um, those two guys who were just in here? Did they say anything funny?"

Ellie looked at him. "Who wants to know?" she asked.

"Uh . . . it's, like, a bet we're having," Bradley said. "About their voices."

Ellie shook her head. "They just asked for two hot teas to go," she said. "Oh, and they said Green Lawn has some real nice houses."

Bradley thanked Ellie and hurried outside. *Real nice houses! Thieves always pick nice houses to rob!*

The strangers were standing in front of Furry Feet Pet Shop, looking through the window. The one in the ski mask yanked it up to take a sip of his tea. Then he snapped a picture of the shop.

Bradley stared. The guy in the ski mask was wearing lipstick. It was a

woman! And her face was tanned, too.

Bradley noticed something else. As the woman had taken the camera from her coat pocket, something had fallen out onto the sidewalk.

The man and woman walked away, crossing Oak Street and heading past the post office.

Bradley ran to pick up what the woman had dropped. It was a piece of green paper, folded in half. When Bradley unfolded it, he saw SHANGRI-LA HOTEL printed in fancy letters at the top.

Below that, someone had printed something. Bradley read it quickly, but it didn't make any sense.

"It's like a code," he muttered to himself. *"A secret burglar code!"*

3

The Secret Code

Brian, Nate, and Lucy came sprinting across the street.

Bradley told them what Ellie had said and showed them the note. "The woman dropped it," he said.

"What woman?" his brother asked.

Bradley pointed at the two strangers, who were now passing the post office. "The short one is a woman. I saw her lipstick!"

Nate squinted. "Or it's a man pretending to be a woman!" he said. "Thieves are so tricky!"

"And they both have tans," Bradley added.

"I'll bet it's makeup!" Nate said. "To fool the police!"

Brian, Nate, and Lucy huddled around Bradley, peering at the paper.

WLK N 2 G.L.E.S.
E ON WDY 2 D & H
N ON FRM LN 2 P

"This is just a bunch of initials," Nate said. "It might as well be written in a foreign language!"

Lucy took the note from Bradley. "Do you think they're staying at the Shangri-la Hotel?" she said.

"I don't think thieves stay at hotels in the same town where they're robbing houses," Nate said. "They just steal stuff, then take off!"

"But if they're not staying at the hotel, how did they get this Shangri-la Hotel paper?" Brian asked.

"Maybe they stole it!" Bradley said. "Mr. Linkletter keeps some on his desk."

"What does it mean?" Nate asked.

"It's like a word puzzle," Lucy said. "I have a book of these. See, most of the vowels are missing."

"The *D, H,* and *P* are underlined," Brian said. "But none of the other letters are."

"It's a burglar's code," Bradley whispered.

"Guys, they're walking toward the bank!" Brian said. "We have to keep following them!"

Lucy gave the mysterious note back to Bradley, and he slipped it into his pocket.

The four kids followed slowly, keeping the two strangers in sight.

"That tall guy is weird," Brian said.

"Before, his left leg was limping, but now it's his right leg!"

"Are you sure?" Lucy asked.

Brian tapped his head. "I never forget a limper!" he said.

"Hold it!" Bradley whispered. The kids crouched behind a row of bushes in front of the post office. "They're stopping at the bank!"

The two strangers put their faces against the bank windows. Then the man in the cowboy hat pulled a notebook and pencil from a pocket in his backpack. He wrote something and put the notebook away.

The woman took a picture of the bank.

"They're taking more pictures!" Nate said. "We have to do something!"

"Like what?" Lucy asked. "All they're doing is looking."

"Yeah, looking in bank windows

and writing stuff in a notebook and taking pictures," Nate said. "That's what thieves do when they're making a plan!"

The bank clock now read three-thirty. "At least the bank is closed," Brian said. "They can't get in."

"The doors were locked at Mrs. Wong's house, too," Nate said. "But they still got in!"

"We don't know that for sure," Lucy reminded him. "Someone else could have stolen her computer."

"They're on the move again," Nate said. "Let's go."

The kids followed the limping man and the woman in the ski mask farther down Main Street.

The strangers stopped in front of the elderly-housing building. The woman snapped a picture, and the man wrote something in his little notebook. Then they went in.

"Oh my gosh, they're going to rob those old people!" Brian said.

"The police station is next door," Bradley said. "Maybe we should tell Officer Fallon what's going on!"

"But nothing is going on," Lucy said. "Officer Fallon would get mad if we asked him to arrest two innocent people!"

Bradley shook his head. "He'd get madder if they robbed his whole town!" he said.

"So what should we do?" Nate asked.

"Let's just wait a minute," Brian said. "But if we hear anyone scream, we run to the police station, okay?"

They waited, and no one screamed. Three minutes later, an old man and woman came out. They had white hair and walked stooped over. One carried a big shopping bag, and they held on to each other as they walked down the steps.

The four kids watched the old couple shuffle down Main Street.

At the Shangri-la Hotel, one of them opened the bag, took out a camera, and aimed it at the hotel's entrance.

"It's them!" Brian yelled. "The thieves changed into different disguises!"

4

Who Are the Grontses?

"Are you sure?" Bradley said. "Wasn't one of them carrying a backpack?"

"I'll bet it's inside that shopping bag," Nate said. "They must have had extra clothes and wigs in there, too."

"Neither one is limping," Lucy said.

"Ha!" Brian said. "That's one of their tricks. Sometimes they limp, and sometimes they don't!"

"Still think they're just innocent tourists?" Nate asked Lucy.

"I really don't know what to think,"

Lucy muttered under her breath.

The white-haired couple entered the hotel.

"Maybe they're after Mr. Linkletter's computer!" Nate said. "We'd better warn him!"

"But we can't let them know we're following them," Lucy said.

"We can watch them through the door," Bradley said. "They'll never notice us."

The four kids crept up to the thick glass door and peered inside. They saw the old couple talking to Mr. Linkletter at the counter. They were smiling. Then they walked toward the elevators.

"Let's go!" Bradley said. He shoved the door open and the kids piled in.

Mr. Linkletter's eyes got wide when he saw the kids. His eyebrows went up an inch and his mustache twitched.

"Hello, young people," he said. "What

brings you out on New Year's Eve? Are you checking in to our most expensive room?"

Bradley knew Mr. Linkletter was fooling with them. He was always joking around, but you couldn't tell because he almost never smiled.

"We're too young to check in to a hotel," Brian said.

Bradley looked at the counter. There was the sign that said, C. LINKLETTER, MANAGER. There was the little bell that new guests rang when they came in. And there was the neat pile of green paper with SHANGRI-LA HOTEL printed at the top.

Mr. Linkletter nodded. "Indeed," he said. "So how can I help you today?"

"That old couple you were talking to," Nate said. "Are they staying here?"

Mr. Linkletter crossed his arms. "I never discuss my guests," he said. "Why do you want to know?"

"Um, we're playing a game," Nate said.

Mr. Linkletter raised one eyebrow. He waited.

"You see," Nate went on, "we pick someone we don't know, and we follow them. We pretend they're really important, like a movie star or the president."

"Yeah, and we try to guess stuff about them," Brian added.

"It's practice," Nate said, beaming his best smile at Mr. Linkletter. "In case we become detectives when we grow up!"

Bradley looked at his feet so he wouldn't laugh.

"I assure you young, um, *detectives*," Mr. Linkletter said, "that Mr. and Mrs. Gronts aren't movie stars. And they don't live in the White House, either."

He turned the register and put a long finger under a name: MR. A. GRONTS, 1212 TWELFTH STREET, MIAMI, FL.

"Great," Bradley said. "That means I

win the game! I guessed they were from Florida because of their tans!"

"The Grontses are old friends of this hotel," Mr. Linkletter went on. "They come to Green Lawn every Christmas to visit Mr. Gronts's sister, Mabel, who lives in the elderly-housing building."

Bradley grabbed his brother's arm and tugged. "Come on," he whispered.

The kids sat on the sofa across the lobby from the check-in counter.

"I guess I was wrong about those white-haired people," Brian said. "But when she pulled out a camera, I thought they were the thieves."

"But what happened to the two we were following?" Nate asked. "The guy with the limp and the woman with the ski mask? They went into the elderly-housing place, but they didn't come out."

"They're probably still inside, stealing stuff from old people," Brian said.

The kids got quiet.

Bradley took the green note from his pocket and unfolded it on his knee. "Let's try to figure this out," he said.

Lucy put her finger on WLK. "If we put in an A, this becomes WALK," she said.

"Okay, but what about the rest, WLK N 2 G.L.E.S.?" asked Nate.

"How about WALK NORTH?" Bradley said. "And the 2 could mean the word TO. WALK NORTH TO G.L.E.S.?"

"You're a genius!" Brian said. "And if the N stands for NORTH, the E on the second line might be EAST!"

"I get it!" Nate said. "If you add two O's to WDY, it could mean WOODY. We live on Woody Street. WALK EAST ON WOODY TO D AND H. Whatever *that* means."

"Maybe the H stands for your last name, Hathaway," Bradley said.

"And the D could be DUNCAN," Lucy said. "Or DINK DUNCAN."

"Then the P could be PINTO, our last name!" Brian said. He looked at the note, then said, "If you add three A's and an E, you get: WALK NORTH ON FARM LANE TO PINTO."

Bradley looked at the other kids. "I think I get this," he said in a low voice. "The thieves wrote down directions to our houses! I'll bet they planned to rob all of us! They checked out your house first, Nate. When they saw us through the window, they ran away."

"Right, so they decided to go to Dink's house next door," Nate said. "But they saw us watching them, so they took off."

"Where are they going next?" Bradley asked. He looked at the note again. "To this G.L.E.S. place?"

"How much do you want to bet that G.L.E.S. stands for Green Lawn Elementary School?" Brian asked. "They're going to rob our school!"

"There are lots of computers there," Nate said.

"And it's closed for the holiday, so no one would notice they were stolen," Bradley said.

"Maybe they're at the school right now!" Brian said.

"But we saw them go into that elderly-housing building," Lucy reminded them. "Why don't we just go in and ask about them?"

"Good idea!" Bradley said.

The four kids waved at Mr. Linkletter and left the hotel. They passed the town hall and marched into the home for elderly people. A woman with white hair and pink cheeks greeted them from behind a desk. "May I help you, dear?" she asked Nate.

Nate smiled at the woman. "We're looking for a man and a woman who came in here a few minutes ago," he said.

"He was tall and had a ponytail," Lucy said.

"And a limp," Brian added.

"He was with a short woman with a ski mask on her face," Bradley said.

The woman's eyes grew wide. "Yes, they came in here, and they acted very mysterious!" she said.

"They did?" Bradley asked.

"Yes, they were giggling like children," the woman said. "Then they asked me if there was a back door. I pointed to it, and they raced out and disappeared!"

"Did they say anything else?" Nate asked.

"Well, I'm a little hard of hearing," the woman said. "But when they ran past my desk, I think I heard the woman say, 'Fix the clock, Artie.'"

The kids just looked at her.

"Fix what clock?" Brian asked.

"And who's Artie?" Nate said.

"I'm sure I have no idea," the old

woman said. "Our clock is working just fine! My brother is named Arthur, but no one calls him Artie!"

"Can we go out the back door, too?" Bradley asked the woman.

"Of course, dear," she said, watching the kids tear down the hallway. "Goodness, everyone is in such a hurry!"

The kids ran outside. No one was

there. The falling snow was covering the back-door steps.

"If there were any footprints, they're hidden under the snow," Brian said. He looked over a short fence at the police station next door. "I'll bet the thieves didn't go *there*!"

"Well, where *did* they go?" Lucy asked.

The kids stared into the falling snow. It was getting darker. They could hear music coming from Main Street. People were getting ready to celebrate New Year's Eve.

"I guess we'd better go home," Bradley said. "For the six o'clock party."

"What did you say?" Lucy asked Bradley.

"Mom wants us home before six o'clock," Bradley said. "For the party."

"Six o'clock party," Lucy muttered. "Oh my gosh, what if that's what she heard?"

"What if what is what who heard?" Brian asked, shaking his head.

Lucy wiped some snow off her face. "The woman inside said she heard one of the thieves say 'Fix the clock, Artie.'"

The boys looked at her. "So?" Nate said.

"Well, what if that was wrong?" Lucy asked. "What if the woman said 'Six o'clock party' and not 'Fix the clock, Artie'?"

The boys stared at Lucy.

"You think they're coming to our party?" Brian asked. "Why would they do that?"

"To rob you!" Nate said. "To tie us all up in the barn and take all your Christmas presents!"

Lucy nodded. "The crooks know where we live, right?" she asked. "That note Bradley found had directions to each house. They tried Nate's first. Then they spied on Dink's house. So now—"

"That's where they went when they ran out this back door!" Bradley said. "North on Farm Lane to P. And P is for Pinto. That's us!"

"But we don't have anything to steal," Brian said. "My piggy bank is empty, and—"

"Laptops, bro!" Bradley said. "Josh has one. Mom has one. Dad got a new one for Christmas. They took Mrs. Wong's, and now they're after ours!"

"But how do the crooks know we have laptops?" Brian asked.

"And how do they know about the party?" Nate asked. "Are these crooks mind readers, too?"

"If we're right about them, they could be part of a ring of thieves," Lucy said. "My dad told me about some thieves in California. The leaders send their crooks all over the country. In California, they were after gold. They'd break into houses and look for jewelry like rings and charm bracelets."

"Come on," Bradley said. "Let's head home. If they come, we'll be ready for them!"

5

Sneaking Up on the Thieves

The kids crossed Main Street and cut behind Howard's Barbershop. Lots of people were out in the snow. Some big kids were having a snowball fight. A few other kids were building a snow fort behind the Book Nook. A man was walking his dog. The dog was wearing a green sweater with tiny bells sewn all over it. When the dog walked, the bells jingled. Everybody except the dog had a red nose and shiny eyes.

The kids passed the high school and the swan pond.

"Where do swans go in winter?" Brian asked.

"They fly to Florida," Bradley said.

"In an airplane?" Nate joked. "It would be fun sitting in an airplane next to a big white swan!"

They came to Woody Street. There were lights on in Dink's house and in Nate's house. The kids peeked in the windows to make sure there were no burglars prowling around.

Bradley pulled out the note and looked at it again. "North on Farm Lane to P," he said as they left Woody Street. They hiked up Farm Lane, leaving footprints in the snow.

"We should sneak up on our house," Brian said. "Maybe we'll catch them in the act!"

A few minutes later, they stood in Bradley and Brian's front yard. It was almost dark, and snow was floating down in big, wet flakes. Lights were on in every room of the house. Behind the house, the barn stood dark and cold-looking.

"I see big footprints," Bradley whispered, pointing at the ground.

"They're probably Josh's," Brian said. "He has giant feet."

The kids walked up onto the porch, trying to be as quiet as mice. They peered through the windows at Bradley and Brian's living room. A fire was in the fireplace, and a Christmas tree stood in one corner. Pal was lying in front of the fireplace, sound asleep.

"There are Mom and Dad," said Bradley.

Everyone was wearing a party hat with HAPPY NEW YEAR! printed on the front. Bradley's dad had on oversize yellow sunglasses.

"And my aunt and uncle," Lucy said.

"Dink, Josh, and Ruth Rose are

frosting cupcakes!" Nate said. "Let's go in and help them!"

Just then, Nate's parents walked out of the kitchen into the living room. Mr. and Mrs. Hathaway were wearing party hats, too, and carrying a banner. They hung it from the fireplace mantel. In gold letters, it said: HAPPY NEW YEAR!

"It's going to be a fun party," Nate said. "Why am I standing out in the cold with my nose running?"

"Because you're going to help catch two laptop thieves," Bradley reminded Nate.

"But they're not here," Lucy said.

"Maybe they came, but when they saw how many people were in there, they got chicken and left," Nate said.

"Let's go in," Bradley said. "We can't stay out here all night."

The four kids banged in through the front door. They shook snow off their

hats, pulled off their coats, and kicked their boots into a corner.

"You're here!" Bradley's mom cried. "We thought you'd been kidnapped and taken to the North Pole!"

"Cool!" Josh said, grinning. He had green frosting on his lips. "More cupcakes for us!"

"Your cheeks are so pink," Dink's mother said. "You look like you're freezing! Come and sit by the fire."

"Good thing you guys showed up," Dink said. "We were getting ready to go out looking for you."

"Where were you, Nate?" Ruth Rose asked her brother. "I called our house an hour ago, but no one answered. You were supposed to stay there."

"We were following a gang of thieves!" Nate answered.

"You were *what*?" his father demanded.

"Mrs. Wong's laptop got stolen out

of her house," Bradley explained. Everyone was staring at him and the other younger kids. "Then the thieves came to Nate's house and peeked in the window. We followed them all over town, but we lost them."

"We think they're coming here next!" Brian whispered. "Show them the note, Bradley."

Bradley produced the note. "See, they had directions to all our houses!"

"Well, they're not here," said his mother. "All our laptops are safe." She handed the kids hats with rubber bands that went under their chins. Each hat said HAPPY NEW YEAR! in bright colors.

Bradley, Brian, Nate, and Lucy put the hats on, grinning at each other.

"Who wants hot chocolate?" Bradley's dad asked.

Everyone raised a hand, and the adults went into the kitchen.

"I challenge you guys to Scrabble," Josh said. "We'll play in teams, boys against girls!"

"No fair," Lucy said. "There are only two girls and five boys!"

"But the girls are smarter," Ruth Rose said. "Lucy and I will cream you guys!"

The seven kids sprawled on the floor around the Scrabble board. They sipped hot chocolate. The fire snapped and the clock ticked. Pal snored.

Josh excused himself. "Be right back," he said. "Don't cheat!"

A minute later, Dink left, too. "Back in a second," he said.

After another minute, Ruth Rose stood up, stretched, and left the room. "Don't drink my hot chocolate, Nate," she said.

The fire snapped. The clock ticked. Pal had left with Ruth Rose.

"Where are they?" Nate asked. "It's Josh's turn."

Bradley got up and walked into the kitchen. He came right back out. "They're gone. All our parents have disappeared, too," he said. He looked around the room. "Even Pal is gone. We're all alone."

"Except for the thieves," Brian said in a spooky voice.

6

A Light in the Barn

"I'll bet Mom and Dad and the others went for a walk," Bradley said. "Grown-ups love to walk in the dark."

"But what about the party? And why didn't they say anything?" Brian asked.

"We were busy playing Scrabble," Nate said. He looked at the wall clock. "Six o'clock."

"Time for the thieves to come," Brian joked. "Maybe they'll steal Nate instead of a laptop. Maybe they'll—"

Lucy stood up and looked out the

window. "Guys, there's a light on in your barn," she whispered. "I saw it in one of the windows."

The three boys jumped up. They peered out into the dark backyard at the barn.

"Nah, it's just a reflection from the lights in the house," Bradley said.

Brian ran around and shut off all the lights. The light in the barn was still glowing.

"The light is moving!" he said.

"Oh my gosh, it *is* the thieves!" Nate said. "Run for cover!"

"We're not running anywhere!" Bradley announced. "This is our house and that's our barn!"

They huddled in front of the window, all eyes on the barn.

"Why would the crooks be in our barn?" Bradley asked. "There's nothing out there but Polly and a bunch of junk."

"Polly!" Brian yelped. "Maybe they got bored with stealing laptops, and now they're after ponies!"

"The light is moving again!" Nate said.

A small glow passed from window to window in the barn.

"Someone is walking around out there!" Brian said. "Maybe they *are* taking Polly!"

"Grab your coats!" Bradley yelled, jumping up. "Nobody steals the Pinto pony!"

The kids scrambled into their coats and boots. "But what are we supposed to do?" Nate asked. "Those two thieves are big, and we're just little kids!"

"We can at least look through the windows," Bradley said. "If we see them in there, we call Officer Fallon. I don't care if it *is* New Year's Eve!"

Bradley opened the back door. "Walk like mice on ice!" he whispered.

The four kids tiptoed single file across the backyard. The moon shone down, creating shadows on the snow.

"Look at these big footprints!" Bradley whispered. "They all lead straight to the barn!"

The kids studied the footprints, then crept toward the barn door.

"Guys, what's that?" Lucy asked, pointing. A dark lump sat on the snow a few feet from the closed barn door.

Bradley peered at the object. "Everything else is covered with snow," he whispered.

Lucy took a few steps closer.

"Don't touch it!" Nate cried. "It could be a skunk! They come out at night!"

"It doesn't have a white stripe, and it's not moving," Lucy said. She walked over and picked up the object.

"It's a ski mask," Lucy whispered. "It's the one that woman thief was wearing. She must have dropped it here!"

"So that must be them in the barn," Bradley whispered. "Let's go."

The kids ran quietly to the side of the barn. Brian and Bradley dragged a bench under one of the windows. All four kids climbed onto the bench and peeked into the barn.

Their breath fogged the glass, and Bradley wiped it away. "Do you see anyone?" he asked, barely whispering.

"Dad's lantern is lit on the workbench," Brian said. "But no thieves."

"I see Polly, but she's not in her stall," Lucy said. "She's just standing in the middle of the barn, eating hay."

"Josh must have let her out of her stall," Bradley said. "Let's try a different window." They carried the bench to the next window and climbed up for another look.

"The same," Nate said. "Nothing."

They moved the bench again, this time around the corner to the back of the barn. But when they stood on the bench and peered through the glass, they couldn't see anything. Something tall and pink was blocking their view.

"What the heck is that?" Brian asked. "We don't have anything tall and pink."

"It's standing right in front of the window," Nate said.

"There's a ribbon on it," Lucy said. "Maybe it's a big Christmas present for you guys."

"Christmas was last week," Bradley said. He jumped off the bench. "Come on. We're going in," he said.

"Are you sure?" Nate asked. "What if we went back to your house and played Scrabble instead?"

Brian clapped Nate on the shoulder. "What's the matter—don't you like surprises?" he asked.

"Not like this," Nate said. "It could be anything. Like a pink monster that eats children!"

"So while it's chewing on *you,* we'll run to our house and eat all the cupcakes," Brian cracked.

"Very funny," Nate said.

Brian, Nate, and Lucy followed Bradley around to the front of the barn. The solid wooden door was big and heavy.

"It slides to the side," Bradley whispered. "Let's all pull it open on *three.* One, two, three!"

The door slid open, making a creaking noise. A pigeon flapped its wings above their heads. Polly let out a soft whinny.

"Is anybody h-here?" Bradley asked the dark, empty space.

Nobody answered.

"Look," Nate said. He was pointing toward the other end of the barn. The pink object was a box at least six feet tall.

"A giant box," Bradley said.

"With a ribbon on it," Lucy said. "And a big bow on top."

"I've never seen such a giant present," Bradley said. "Should we open it?"

"No way!" Nate said. "It could be filled with rats or snakes or a million bloodsucking spiders!"

"It could be filled with a million pieces of candy," Brian said. He headed for the pink present, and the others followed him.

7

The Giant Pink Box

But the kids never made it. As they passed Polly's stall, the door flew open. A bunch of people burst out of the stall, yelling, "SURPRISE!" Pal was suddenly there, running in circles and barking like mad.

Dink, Josh, and Ruth Rose began throwing streamers and confetti all over Lucy. "HAPPY BIRTHDAY, LUCY!" everyone yelled. "HAPPY BIRTHDAY! HAPPY NEW YEAR!"

Bradley's mouth fell open.

Brian's mouth fell open.

Nate's mouth fell open.

Lucy began to cry.

Everyone gathered around Lucy, giving her birthday hugs. Officer Fallon was there, and Mr. Linkletter. Even he was smiling at Lucy. Ellie was there, and Mrs. Wong, with her tall nephew, Leonard. Josh was grinning like a monkey, standing with Dink and Ruth Rose.

Bradley looked at his parents and Dink's and Nate's parents. "You tricked us!" he said.

"Yes, we did," his mother said. "And it was fun!"

"I thought this was supposed to be a New Year's Eve party," Brian said.

"It is, but it's also for Lucy's birthday!" her aunt said. "We're celebrating both."

"Cool!" Nate said. "So why is she crying?"

"I know why," Ruth Rose said. "She misses her parents. Right, Lucy?"

Lucy nodded. She tried to smile, but the tears kept coming.

"Well, she'll feel better when she opens her present," Bradley's mother said, pointing at the tall pink box. "Here are some scissors. Cut the paper, Lucy."

Lucy took the scissors and walked up to the pink present. It was three feet taller than she was. "Where should I cut?" she asked. "It's so big!"

"Let me help you," Josh said. He stepped over and made a big rip right in the middle. Then Dink and Ruth Rose came over. They began ripping all the paper. Underneath was cardboard, and they tore that off, too.

Then Lucy screamed.

Out of the ripped box stepped a tall man in a cowboy hat. The woman with him no longer wore the ski mask.

"Mommy! Daddy!" Lucy yelled. "You came!"

Everyone in the barn began whistling and laughing and yelling, "Happy birthday, Lucy!"

"Of course we came!" Lucy's mother said. "We would never miss your birthday!"

Lucy's father scooped Lucy up and gave her a big hug. "I guess I can stop limping now," he said.

"Well, I'll be a kangaroo's cousin," Nate said. "It was them all the time!"

"We had fun leading you kids all over town," Lucy's mother said.

"And everybody knew?" Bradley asked.

"We certainly knew," Mr. Linkletter said. "But we love keeping secrets in Green Lawn!"

"The only ones who were clueless were you four!" Josh said. "Dink and Ruth Rose and I knew all week!"

"We got to go to the airport yesterday to pick up your parents," Ruth Rose told Lucy.

"But . . . but . . . so there was never a burglar at all?" Nate said. He looked at Mrs. Wong. "No one stole your laptop?"

"Oh, someone took it all right," Mrs. Wong said. "My big, sweet nephew took my laptop to be cleaned, as my Christmas present. But he never told me!"

Leonard blushed. "Yeah, it was supposed to be a surprise for Aunt Mary," he said.

"So everyone was looking for a burglar who didn't exist," Officer Fallon said.

"But why were you guys peeking in places and taking pictures?" Nate asked Lucy's parents.

"We're going to make a scrapbook for Lucy," her mother said. "So we took pictures and made notes about Green Lawn."

"We decided to have some fun with you," Lucy's dad said, giving Lucy a squeeze. "So we acted like mysterious strangers doing weird things. But we didn't know you'd mistake us for burglars!"

"Daddy stuck on the ponytail and made up the limp so you wouldn't recognize him," Lucy's mother said.

"Yeah, but he changed legs!" Brian said.

Lucy's father laughed. "You noticed that?" he asked.

"But what about when you changed your disguises?" Bradley asked. "You dressed as old people with white hair, and we followed you to the hotel! We saw you go up in an elevator!"

Lucy's father and mother looked confused. "What old people?"

Mr. Linkletter made a small cough. "I told you that was Mr. and Mrs. Gronts," he said. "They would be amused to know that you suspected them of being New Year's Eve thieves!"

"So who's hungry?" Bradley's dad asked. "There's a huge cake inside with Lucy's name on it!"

Everyone cheered. They all trooped out of the barn toward the house.

Bradley, Brian, Nate, and Lucy walked together at the back of the group.

"So how do you feel now, Lucy?" Nate asked.

"Awesome!" Lucy said. "I never in a million years thought my parents were hiding in that box!"

"Me either," Nate said. "I was hoping for the candy."